Assignments
for a Season

Assignments for a Season

Assignments
for a Season

Debbie Patrick

Assignments for a Season
by Debbie Patrick

Copyright © 2022. All rights reserved. No part of this book may be reproduced or transmitted in any form or by any means, electronic or mechanical, including photocopying, recording or by any information storage and retrieval system without the written permission of the author or publisher, except for the inclusion of brief quotations in a review or article, when credit to the book, author, publisher, and order information are included in the review or article.

ISBN 978-1-954509-05-4

Printed in the United States of America

Scripture marked (CEV) are taken from the CONTEMPORARY ENGLISH VERSION. Copyright ©1995, by the American Bible Society. Used by permission. All rights reserved.

Scripture marked ESV are taken from *THE HOLY BIBLE, ENGLISH STANDARD VERSION*®. Copyright © 2001 by Crossway, a publishing ministry of Good News Publishers. Used by permission.

Scripture marked (NAS) are taken from the NEW AMERICAN STANDARD BIBLE®. Copyright © 1960, 1962, 1963, 1968, 1971, 1972, 1973, 1975, 1977, 1995 BY THE LOCKMAN FOUNDATION. Used by permission. All rights reserved.

Cover illustration by Danny Wilson, dannywilson.com
Staff shift transition prayer on page 27 taken from *Every Moment Holy*, Volume 1, by Douglas Kaine McKelvey.

Assignments for a Season

Dedication

To all the hard-working staff members at Dominion Senior Living. We appreciate you.

Assignments for a Season

Preface

The story that follows is fiction, although it is inspired by real life. The characters, names, places, and situations are works of fiction. Any resemblance to actual persons, places, or events, living or dead, is purely accidental — although the author believes the loving attitudes of compassionate care exhibited among the characters are very real.

Assignments for a Season

Acknowledgments

With any book project, there are so many people to thank. First, Peter Hall and Augie Barker of Dominion Senior Living, who envisioned this project; to Grant Standefer and Alan Shipley who arranged for numerous on-site visits, introductions and meetings with Dominion Senior Living associates and staff, and their generous contributions of time, wisdom, and insights.

To the many, many friends, family, and interns who proofed, corrected, and suggested edits and changes, you know who you are, and I am indebted to your efforts.

To Steve Hall, who set the course of the amazing faith-based culture at Dominion through Empire Construction: I am inspired by the depth to which you, through your many companies and endeavors, practice exactly what you preach.

Assignments for a Season

Contents

Preface 7

Acknowledgments 8

Chapter 1 - Sara Johnson, CNA 13

Chapter 2 - Nancy's Move-In Day 21

Chapter 3 - Getting Acquainted 35

Chapter 4 - Going with God's Flow 45

Chapter 5 - Everyday Service and Sacrifice 59

Chapter 6 - Challenges Come When a Family Gathers.. 75

Chapter 7 - Finishing Well 79

Chapter 8 - Sara's Thoughts 87

Epilogue 93

About the Author 95

Dominion Senior Living 97

End Notes 101

Assignments for a Season

Chapter 1: Sara Johnson, CNA

Chapter 1

Sara Johnson, CNA
Lakeview Senior Care

It was hard for her to hold back the tears. She always tried to put on a brave face at work; however, her thoughts were such a different story. They kept going, circling over and over Mrs. Nancy's life and the time they'd spent together. *You always found meaning and lessons in the most ordinary things, didn't you?* She thought, as she folded clean clothes and pretended she was still talking to her friend. She didn't think of *all* of the residents as her friends, but most were, and Mrs. Nancy had been one of her favorites. Sara was now folding the freshly laundered residents' clothes with a vengeance. *I know it's part of the job,* she reminded herself, *but I just hate it. And it never gets any easier.*

Assignments for a Season

Especially losing Nancy.

Sara knew she had to keep going, keep putting one foot in front of the other, keep looking after all the other residents as if her whole life hadn't changed. She was a professional, after all, but losing Nancy had been almost like losing her Grannie all over again. Though they weren't blood-kin, and Mrs. Nancy hadn't been here much more than a year, she was a wise, wonderful, giving woman who graced Sara's life toward the end of hers, and left a crater-sized hole in her wake.

Meanwhile, there were 60 other residents and a full staff grieving the loss as well. As always, they'd pull together, pray and grieve together, and God would get them through. *What would we do without His amazing grace? We'll need it in large doses today, Lord!* She half thought, half prayed. She shook her head in wonder. Yes, God always met her right where she was, and pulled her through to the other side of whatever the situation was. Her marriage. Her kids. Anything in life — including death.

Deep in thought, Sara realized she'd been working here at Lakeview Senior Care for 13 years. She'd been just out of Tech, with her newly minted CNA certification — a Certified Nurses Assistant. She had been so proud, ready to take on the world, and most days, she still could. In the years since, Sara had gotten married and had two children. She'd seen many residents come, and too many of them go on to their heavenly homes. Her position required navigating the sometimes tricky relationships with residents' family members both when

Chapter 1: Sara Johnson, CNA

they were happy and when they were not. She also fought valiantly to keep all the community safe, sometimes even from their own families, particularly when they'd had a bout of that devastating COVID-19 virus a few years back. The whole country went on lockdown for over a year — two before things seemed anywhere close to normal again. As contagious as that virus was, they had mostly dodged the bullets. Three residents and two staff members tested positive, but they were able to quarantine without it spreading further. During that time the residents and staffers were frustrated with all the new safety rules to follow, and family members were furious when told they couldn't visit. Now the danger had mostly passed, and everyone understood that for safety's sake, it was not just housekeeping, but everybody's job to keep the residents safe and clean, personally and environmentally. With the vulnerabilities of elderly residents, she and the rest of the staff were on the front lines, shouldering the responsibility for protecting them.

But today, Sara felt uncharacteristically worn out, mentally and emotionally. She felt the weight of being a single parent, and in her sadness, wished Jeremy could just put his arms around her, kiss her head and tell her it was all going to be okay. She longed to sink into his big chest and shoulders, wrapped in one of his massive hugs. Funny how she used to feel so safe and comforted with him around. She wished that he was still the man she'd fallen in love with… the one she'd married and dreamed of a future with. Wistfully she remembered all the possibilities she'd once seen ahead of them, how she thought they would have a wonderful life together. Even now after all he'd put her through, some days the sight of him could still make her heart skip a beat.

But she loved her children even more than Jeremy. She had a responsibility to them, and when Jeremy was using or even just drinking it wasn't safe for any of them to be around him. *God bless him, Lord, I wish you'd get ahold of that man!* She looked toward the ceiling, as if searching visibly for God, transferring the conversation in her head directly toward Him. *There's so much good in Jeremy when he's clean. It is such a waste of a life, the way he's going. Please help him, if not for me then for the kids.*

She sighed. She knew it was out of her hands. Once more she mentally laid that issue down and left it with God. Again. *"Didn't cause it, can't control it, can't cure it,"* she repeated to herself. Even though she had started attending the twelve-step program for families of addicts in order to help her children, what she was learning there was helping her too. She was learning when to take action, and when to step back and leave it with God. This was one of those leave it to God moments. Oh, how she sometimes hated that! But there was no action she could take that would help, except to wait and pray. It was out of her hands.

Sara straightened her shoulders and began taking laundry bundles back to the residents' rooms. She paused outside Mrs. Field's door, took a deep breath and put on her brightest smile.

Chapter 1: Sara Johnson, CNA

"How you doing this morning, Beautiful? It's time to rise and shine," she said brightly, as she started putting away the clean clothes. "Do you need help getting ready for breakfast?"

Mrs. Fields was still trying to wake up. Her hair was disheveled and pajamas rumpled as she sat on the edge of her bed. She half smiled as Sara started laying out her clothes for the day.

"Oh, I'm doing alright. Just give me a minute to get my bearings. I don't think I'll need any help — but could you just bring me my walker from the corner over there," she said, gesturing toward the far corner of her room.

"Sure thing," said Sara, breathing a private sigh of relief that Mrs. Fields was beginning the day in a good mood. She would give her a few minutes to wake up before returning to get her for breakfast.

Sara returned to the laundry, to collect and deliver more clean clothes and more wake up calls. Then she'd need to help Mrs. Rhonda with her shower; she wanted a shower every morning before breakfast and always needed help with both bathing and getting dressed.

Mrs. Rhonda had lived all over the world as a diplomat's wife, and she was very particular about her grooming and presentation. She wouldn't let the staff do her laundry. She insisted everything be sent out to the dry cleaners. Sara continued her thoughts. *Goodness, Mrs. Rhonda's clothes! She always dressed "to the nines" as Grannie used to say. I'm not sure what that really meant, except that you were really something fancy if you were dressed to the nines. That was Mrs. Rhonda, every single day. I wonder what would happen if she ever just let her hair down and went casual. I can't even imagine.* She laughed at the thought.

Soon enough, all the residents were up and in the dining room, seated, served, and chatting about the day ahead. Sara took the opportunity to get a cup of coffee and head to the break room.

"How's it going, girlfriend?" Katie asked Sara as soon as she walked in. "Are you okay?" Katie Gold was a Residents Assistant (RA) that worked with Sara. Except for their jobs, they had little in common, but the women had become good friends. Katie could read Sara like a book, and she knew just from seeing her that Sara was having a hard day.

Sara smiled. It was good to have a friend that knew her so well. "Oh I'm getting by." They both knew that grief hung in the room, like a giant elephant that everyone sees, but doesn't mention. Sara sighed and dropped her shoulders, finally saying what everyone was thinking: "I am sure gonna miss that woman. I just can't quite get it through my head that she's gone."

"I know. Same here. She was something special. Unfortunately, Bill and I toasted to her memory a few too many times last night," Katie said, rubbing her temple and acknowledging a bit of a headache.

"You goofball! You don't even drink," Sara laughed at her friend's distress. "Boneheaded move, girl, but I understand."

Chapter 1: Sara Johnson, CNA

"I know! It just seemed like the thing to do, and when Bill suggested it, I went along. We were out until midnight while he listened to all my Mrs. Nancy stories. He really was sweet and understanding," Katie explained.

"That's a new one for him. But yeah, I've been replaying those stories to myself as well. She just — she always knew exactly what to say. She was so encouraging."

"I want to be like Nancy when I grow up," Katie confided.

"Me too," Sara agreed. "Me too." After a long pause she added, "I remember the day she moved in like it was yesterday."

Assignments for a Season

Chapter 2

*Nancy's Move-In Day
Sixteen months earlier —*

"Mom, I get it, this place is beautiful, but it's so far away! There are places just as nice that are so much closer to Joe and me and the kids," Susanne said as she pushed her mother's wheelchair down the hall to what was to become her new home. Her husband, Joe, followed with the luggage and a few boxes packed on a two-wheeled hand truck. Frustrated between guilt, worry, and more than a little relief, Susanne felt she needed to make one last plea.

On one hand, her mother did need more help than she could reasonably give her by herself. After all, she still had to work.

With two kids not too far away from their college years, they needed every dime they could save. But her mother insisted on this senior community back in North Carolina, where she and her dad had moved about 10 years ago. Susanne and her family lived in Tennessee — a good seven hours' drive away. Geographically, it just didn't make sense.

Granted, Lakeview City was a sweet little town, and her parents had fallen in love with it. They were well-rooted in the community, and Susanne knew her father's memory was more alive to her mother here. As for her mother's new "home," Lakeview Senior Care was a beautiful property overlooking the Tar River. It was spotlessly clean and well decorated. It had the look and feel of an upscale apartment complex, rather than what one used to think of an "old folks' home." No, this wasn't some creaky, old manor. It was almost new. The hallway grab bars were concealed to look like chair rail molding, the wallpaper and paint colors were elegant, and everywhere you looked had been tastefully furnished without being too fussy or austere. The ceilings were high, which made both the rooms and public areas seem larger and grander than they actually were. There was lots of natural light from the large windows, too. If one was going to live in a senior community, this was certainly among the strongest options.

"Suze, we talked about this," Nancy answered her daughter, firmly but patiently. "We agreed to disagree. I've got a life here, with my church and my friends. It's home. And you and Joe have your own lives. We tried that." Then she paused, as if

Chapter 2: Nancy's Move-In Day

hesitant to add to her case. Then she softly said, "And honey, it's my decision."

Since her husband's death a year ago, Nancy had uprooted her life, living six months at a time with two of her three surviving adult children. She couldn't continue disrupting both their lives and hers with all that moving. She felt like a burden, and she didn't want that. Neither of their homes felt like home to her, and just about the time they all settled into some kind of workable routine, it was time to move again. Living here at Lakeview was much better. She'd be back around her friends, those she knew from her old neighborhood, and her church family, and it would be hers. For better or worse, it was her new life, for her new season. She was more excited about it than she wanted her family to know. Hers was a small room, to be sure, compared to the lovely home she'd shared with Tad. But it was a place of her own.

∽

In the recreation room down the hall from Nancy's room, Life Enrichment Director Kristin was working hard to keep the residents both entertained and moving. "Now we're going to play cornhole," she told her small group of participants.

They'd just finished singing songs, and now she wanted them to have a little more physical activity. She'd planned the game with indoor boards because it would help exercise their hand-eye coordination and focus. Besides, it would be fun.

Miss Sally groaned loudly. "I hate cornhole," she said. "I'm never any good at it. Can't we do something else?"

One or two of the others nodded to agree and watched cautiously for Kristin's reaction.

She was undeterred.

"Miss Sally," Kristin said, "How are you ever going to get better at it if you never play? Come on, why don't you even go first. Here's a corn bag — just toss it over there to the hole. You'll see — it's really fun." She smiled and pressed the small bag filled with corn feed into Miss Sally's hand.

Instead of tossing the bag at the slanted board, Miss Sally threw it straight down on the floor with all the force she could muster.

"No! I said I don't want to. I won't! And you can't make me you little witch!" Sally shouted, then turned and stomped away, as quickly as her wobbly legs and cane would allow.

The others looked down at the floor or out the recreation room windows toward the river. Anywhere but at what had just taken place.

Kristin tried to maintain her composure. Her face had turned red — she couldn't help that, but she took a deep breath and went on.

"Would anyone else like to play?" She held up the bag, offering it to anyone who would take it. After an awkward silence, one woman raised her hand.

Chapter 2: Nancy's Move-In Day

"I'll take a swing at it dear," offered Rhonda, getting out of her chair to take the corn bag.

"George, do you want to come beat me again?" She grinned. Everyone chuckled as George stood to accept the challenge.

God bless her! Kristin thought to herself. She knew she needed to go apologize to Miss Sally and check on her. But first, she needed to make sure activities continued here for everyone else.

Thanks to Rhonda, ever the diplomat, things were back on an even keel.

Surely arts and crafts this afternoon would be better.

When the games were over, Kristin reminded the group it was just about time for lunch in case anyone needed to freshen up first. She would see them in the dining room. Then she went to find Miss Sally.

After smoothing things over, she retreated to the break room.

"Things going a little better today?" Sara asked.

"Not at all! I tried to get Miss Sally to play cornhole, and instead of playing, she started yelling at me, then stomped off in a huff," Kristin sighed. "I just can't read her — I should have seen it coming. But I didn't.

"She's probably going to report me for trying to get her to do something. It's really discouraging. And honestly, I didn't think I was pushing too hard. I just wanted her to get involved in something. Anything."

"She can be a challenge," Sara agreed. "When I first got here, we had our run-ins, too. She let me know she was in charge of herself, not me or anyone else. We were merely here to <u>*assist*</u> her," she said, laughing. "Once we got that settled, we started to get along pretty well. She'll come around to you too. Just give it some time."

"You really think so?"

"Oh sure. But if you're worried about her reporting you — go talk to Director Rachael about it yourself first, so she's prepared. You could bring it up at prayer time, too, without naming names."

The staff always started their shifts with a meeting, where they shared both essential information about the residents' needs and prayer requests of their own. Then they prayed about all of it and began their workdays. The company owners were deeply faithful. Staff members didn't have to share that faith, but they needed to be respectful of others when they expressed their faith openly. It made the community a unique place to work.

The prayer said by each shift, each day:

My Gift

Today is a day given to me; to love and labor

For our community of seniors.

Let me be united with my teammates, in spirit and purpose,

Chapter 2: Nancy's Move-In Day

With patience, kindness and faithfulness.

Let us serve together, encouraging each other

In our day to day tasks, knowing that this service for others

Brings life and grace to all.

"O Spirit of God, now shape our hearts.

O Spirit of God, now guide our hands.

O Spirit of God, now build Your kingdom among us."

(from Every Moment Holy: Volume 1*)*

Kristin had been raised in a Christian home, but never thought much about what she really believed for herself. She just went along with attending church, youth group, and Sunday school all the way through college because she always had, and because all her friends were there. This was her first job after graduation. As Life Enrichment Director, she was responsible for keeping residents as active and involved as they could be, both socially and physically. You could probably call her an activities director. So it frustrated her when her carefully made plans and lists of activities didn't work out. She had a degree in recreational therapy but was finding this position a lot harder than she thought it would be. The residents had such a wide variety of capabilities and capacities, both mentally and physically, that Kristin found it hard to plan activities that would work for everyone. She'd thought cornhole would be a winner for sure. Right now all she was sure of was that they all knew all the words to "You Are My Sunshine." And repeating that song, as they always did—every—single—day was about to drive her mad. But she couldn't imagine telling the whole staff how much she was struggling by asking for prayer. That was way too far outside her comfort zone. Almost as an afterthought, she supposed she could try praying on her own.

Kristin sipped her coffee and tried to find some humor in the moment, but she wasn't there yet. At least Sara had been kind to her. She wasn't so sure, though, that talking to Director Rachael would be a good idea. She didn't want the Executive Director thinking she wasn't up to her job.

∽

About two o'clock that afternoon, Sara finished the shift she'd started early that morning. After attending the shift turnover meeting and prayer time, she clocked out. The kids would be home from school soon, and after a snack and a shower, she might actually have 30 minutes for a quick nap if they didn't need help with homework. *Thank you, Jesus, for Crockpots! Dinner was all but ready. A bag of salad from the fridge, a bag of chips from the pantry, and chili night was done.*

After dinner, she helped the kids with their homework. Then it was bath time, bedtime stories, prayers, and goodnight kisses —

Chapter 2: Nancy's Move-In Day

her favorite time of the day. How God could have blessed her with these two little angels was more than she could fathom. She watched them snuggle down in their beds after she turned out the lights, as she vowed not to let Him down with the responsibility He'd given her to raise them. *Thank you, Lord. Bless them good!*

∽

Two hours before Sara's alarm went off, the phone rang. She tried to will her body to wake from what had been a sound sleep.

"Hello?"

"Hey Baby. Don't hang up, okay?" It was Jeremy, her soon-to-be ex-husband.

"It's three o'clock in the morning," she groaned. "What's going on?"

"Yeah. But this is my one phone call. I need you to come bail me out, Hon. I'm at county lockup."

Oh Sweet Lord, help me, she quickly shot up a prayer while she listened to his pleading. He'd been picked up for dealing again, and they'd found quite a bit of both pot and pills in his car. Of course Jeremy swore it wasn't his, that the cops just had it out for him. He'd get it all straightened out once she paid the bail bondsman and got his car out of the impound lot. And he was going to need a good lawyer, he told her, seemingly oblivious to the time or trouble he was causing. He rattled on like he was going over a list of all the things he needed to get out of this jam he'd gotten into, not realizing it was already too late.

"Seriously?" Sara demanded. "You can barely pay child support regularly, and you want me to find money to bail you out, pay all the fines and fees, AND hire a fancy lawyer?"

Sara and her sponsor in Al-Anon had talked about this possibility. "Enabling," her sponsor had called it, when you *enable* the addict's bad behavior to continue by rescuing them from facing the consequences of their actions. Like calling in sick for them when they're really just hung over. Or getting them off the floor and into bed when they've passed out. Better to let them make their own call to the boss or wake up still on the floor and have to deal with being stiff and sore in the morning.

But with this, if I don't help ... what will happen? He'll sit in jail ... and lose his job ... and the support checks will stop. What then? He'll be really mad too, and that is the scariest part.

"So — you coming?" Jeremy demanded, interrupting her racing thoughts and prayers.

"No, Jeremy. Not now." She tried to sound sure of herself, but she wasn't. "There's not time. I've got no one to stay with the kids, and I have to be at work in a couple of hours."

"Are you kidding me? Don't you dare let me down like this!" Jeremy was screaming into the phone now.

Chapter 2: Nancy's Move-In Day

"I'm sorry. You're just going to have to wait. I've got to think about it."

"I'm not even believing this." *Click.*

Frankly, she thought to herself, *I'm not believing it either.* It was the first time she hadn't dropped everything to run help him. And she knew she still might. For right now, it was time to think of herself and her kids, and Jeremy would just have to wait.

She decided to go ahead and get up because she was going to need some extra quiet time to pray and calm down before waking the kids.

∼

"Good morning, Mrs. Nancy. Is this a good time to talk?" Liz asked, as she entered Nancy's room. Nancy smiled back at her and waived for her to come on in. "I hope you remember me from when we visited you at your home. I'm Liz Crowder, the Director of Nursing. Are you getting settled in okay?"

"Oh, yes, everything is fine. Everyone's been just wonderful," Nancy told her.

Liz explained that she was there to re-confirm Nancy's medical history for her medical chart.

"We want to make sure we take good care of you," Liz said as she started asking questions, making notes and observations to add to her original information. She also wanted to check for the clarity of Nancy's memory. "We're so glad to have you with us. Could you tell me one more time what brought you here?"

"My husband died thirteen months ago. We'd lived here in Lakeview City for about ten years after he retired from the military. We'd been stationed at Ft. Bragg when he got out. After moving all over, Lakeview City just felt like home — a place where we could build a good life together. And we did, until the Lord took him home. I just thank God he didn't suffer. He had a heart attack one morning before breakfast," she paused at the memory, and took a deep breath. Then she continued, as Liz listened carefully, relieved that this story she was telling matched with the original assessment they'd done at her home before the move.

"Without his help, I needed a caregiver. I tried home health, and then felt like the house was too much to handle with just me there. So I sold my home — it was over in Ridgedale — and tried alternating living in my children's homes, staying with one and then the other for six months at a time. It was just too disruptive, for them and for me. And not fair to anyone. I wanted to come home. This is home. I've got good friends in town and at church — I'm still a member at St. Matthew's — and I'm looking forward to just staying put for awhile."

"That's wonderful, Mrs. Nancy. Now about your medical history, specifically your wheelchair …"

Chapter 2: Nancy's Move-In Day

Nancy chuckled. "You know I almost forget about it, it's been with me so long. Years ago I broke my back in a car wreck. I was blessed to survive at all. The doctors called it a miracle, so I vowed I wouldn't let it slow me down, since God obviously had more for me to do." Her mood visibly brightened.

"Yes, I'm sure He does," Liz said, admiring her refreshing attitude toward life. "Now let's take a minute to go over your medications …"

They continued to chat for some time, until there was another knock at the door.

"Can I join this party?" It was Rachael Shapiro, the Executive Director for Lakeview Senior Care. She told Nancy she'd just dropped by to welcome her and make sure she was getting settled in well.

"That's great, Rachael. I was just leaving," Liz said, gathering her notes and standing up to go. "Mrs. Nancy, it has been a real pleasure seeing you again, and I look forward to having you in our community."

Liz left her room feeling good about their new resident and her ability to thrive at Lakeview. She made a note in the chart that Mrs. Nancy would need help getting up, going to bed, and bathing, but was otherwise mentally sharp and quite competent in her self care.

"We have a little tradition we call a room warming welcome for you with all the staff," Rachael explained, producing an empty flower vase. "Sometime during the day tomorrow, each staff member will come by to introduce themselves and bring you a flower for this vase. By the end of the day, you'll have a lovely, colorful bouquet to remind you that, while we're all different in our personalities and gifts and assignments, we're all working together to make your life a little brighter, and want to welcome you to our community, and your new home."

"What a lovely tradition!" Nancy loved flowers and missed all her pots of flowers and plants that used to fill her home, on every table or flat surface she could find.

∼

At dinner that night, they introduced her to the other residents. She sat with Rhonda, George, and Sally, and found both the food and the company to be very good. *Yes, this is going to work out well,* she thought to herself. She wondered what God's next assignment for her would be. As she looked around the dining room, she felt a spirit of peace settle over her. It felt good to be home.

Chapter 3

Getting Acquainted

"Hello, Mrs. Nancy. I'm Jerri Harding, the housekeeper," Jerri greeted Nancy in her most cheerful and outgoing smile. She'd had to learn to do that very deliberately, because she wasn't outgoing at all, but very shy. Over her time at Lakeview, she'd learned that some of the residents were lonely and needed someone to talk to. She tried hard to be aware and attentive to their need for conversation each day as she went about doing her job. It started with an introduction like this one to each new resident as they arrived.

There were a lot of rooms to clean each day, as well as community spaces, so Jerri worked hard to follow a rigorous schedule. She took a lot of pride in keeping the community clean and attractive. It was important for everyone's safety, and beyond that, it made a difference in their quality of life, too.

"Well, come in, I'm pleased to meet you," Nancy smiled at her warmly. Jerri took her welcome flower out of her cleaning cart and added it to Nancy's growing collection in the vase. She waived hello, a little awkwardly, then turned to begin cleaning the room.

"You know that I've just moved in, but how long have you been here?" Nancy asked her.

"Just about three years now. Would you like for me to adjust these blinds for you?" She asked, noticing that the morning sun was shining brightly straight into Nancy's eyes. Then she looked down and noticed the family pictures on the dresser as she began dusting.

"Are these your grandchildren?"

"Yes — the blessings of old age. The youngest one, Emily, has just turned six. The oldest, Thomas, is almost ready for college. They're all growing so fast. They're thoughtful children — some write me notes, and the young ones have their mothers mail me their drawings, and that's nice too. Do you have children?" Nancy asked.

"Yes, I have one, Teresa. She's 27. She still draws me pictures," Jerri said, cocking her head to one side and nodding

Chapter 3: Getting Acquainted

thoughtfully with a smile as if to say, *but that's okay.* "She lives over at the Sunshine Stars Farm and works at the Sertoma shelter."

"Oh I see," said Nancy, realizing Jerri had just told her that Teresa was a special needs adult child. "That's something we have in common, dear. My Winston is gone now, but he was born with Down syndrome. He was high functioning but died fifteen years ago. It's been a long time, but you never forget either the joy they brought, or the hole they leave in your heart."

"I know that joy for a fact," Jerri agreed, thinking of Teresa's playful skip down the sidewalk that morning, as she'd scampered toward the shelter van that would take her to work. "I can't imagine losing her. It must have been so hard for you, losing a child. It's not supposed to be that way."

"Thank you. But you know that life always has a dimension that's hard. Jesus promised us we would have trouble in this world, but He also told us He's overcome the world[1]. I figure that means we're to accept the losses and troubles that come our way, and make the best of it while we focus on Him. My goodness, you have a real gift for cleaning my friend," Nancy said, admiring the way Jerri moved around the room with ease, but didn't miss a thing that needed wiping, dusting, or straightening. Her room and things were freshly unpacked, and now thanks to Jerri they sparkled. Nancy could tell Jerri took real pride in her work.

"I just think that a clean, ordered place helps a smile stay on your face," Jerri said, grinning at having made up a rhyme. "Our outside influences the inside, and if I can help make that better, I'm pleased to do it. That's one lesson I learned raising Teresa. When she was growing up, if her room was clean and orderly, she seemed happier and able to function better, and I think it's just as true for the rest of us."

"Oh, that's a good lesson. God taught me so many lessons through Winston. Raising a special needs child is most certainly an adventurous road to travel," agreed Nancy. "Full of blessings and challenges."

"I wouldn't trade it for a million dollars," agreed Jerri. "But like you, I couldn't have done it without God's help."

"Amen!" Said Nancy. "When I was raising Winston, along with my other three children, people were always telling me, 'God never gives you more than you can handle' but I don't think that's true at all. It was *always* more than I could handle! I think He set it up that way so that I'd have to stay close to Him for help. I think He doesn't give us more than HE can handle, working through us. Then He sends blessings and encouragement along the way. Like the way you've just worked miracles with this room. You've been a real blessing to me, and the day's not even half over. Who knows what else is in store for us both?"

"Yes ma'am."

They continued chatting for a few more minutes while

Chapter 3: Getting Acquainted

Jerri finished cleaning. Jerri shared more about her personal life than she normally would have, particularly with a newer resident, but Nancy was so warm and open. She felt a little lighter when she left her room.

Isn't that just like God, she reflected. Before she'd met Mrs. Nancy, she'd been building up a good bit of anger nursing some resentment toward the staff on third shift. Did they do anything at all? They'd left the break room in a mess, and none of the laundry was started. They didn't even get started on cleaning the tables in the dining room. Jerri loved to clean, and she tried to get along with everyone and be of service where she could. But it really made her mad when she felt others took advantage of that or were lazy in their own responsibilities. Yes, she'd been working up a full head of steam — and then she went into Mrs. Nancy's room. She was so full of light and love. It was easier now for Jerri to put life and work into perspective. She still meant to talk to Rachael about the overnight shift. But she was now also determined not to let it ruin her day. Jerri started humming to herself as she dusted and disinfected the hallway handrails.

∽

"Hi Mrs. Nancy — I'm Katie Gold," she said, slipping into her room and over to the dresser to add her welcome flower to the bunch. They're starting arts and crafts downstairs in the recreation room in about 20 minutes. Would you like for me to take you down there?"

"How nice, yes, thank you, Katie" Nancy repeated, to make sure she'd remember her name. All the new names and faces were beginning to add up, and she wanted to make sure she kept up with them all. "Tell me about yourself, Katie."

"There's not a lot to tell I guess," said Katie. She was used to being the one asking questions, not being asked about herself. "I'm from Lakeview City, I love going to the beach every chance I get, and I really enjoy getting to work with wonderful folks like you." She hoped that didn't sound as corny to Mrs. Nancy as it had to Katie when it came out of her mouth, but it was true. She hated being put on the spot like that. At least she'd said "folks like you" instead of "old people." She'd missed having grandparents growing up, and now she had a whole building full of surrogates to care for. It was a pretty great job when you looked at it that way.

"Do you have family here?" Nancy continued, as if they were just two girlfriends getting to know each other over lunch.

"Yes—well, that is my folks *were* here, but they just moved to Greenville about six weeks ago. Now that's funny because I got my certification there, and they lived here that whole time. Now, I'm back here and they've moved there. Daddy said the job offer was one he just couldn't pass up."

"Life's funny like that sometimes, isn't it?" Nancy said, as Katie pushed her wheelchair into the open elevator and

Chapter 3: Getting Acquainted

pushed the button for the ground floor. "But Greenville's not too far away."

They rode the elevator down to the lower level in silence.

"What about children? Are you married?" Nancy's questions continued as soon as the elevator door opened. They were personal, but she didn't say them in a way that seemed nosy in the gossipy sense. She seemed genuinely interested in getting to know Katie.

"No children, but I hope to, one day. Not married yet either, but I've got a boyfriend. We've been together for about three years."

"Three years? Good gracious child, what's he waiting on? Or is it you that's doing the waiting?" She asked, eyebrows raised as if she were uncovering a mystery.

Before Katie could answer, they'd arrived at Kristin's arts and crafts activity. She waived them over to the table, which was scattered with supplies of glitter, paper, scissors, Popsicle sticks, and glue.

"That's a question for another day," Katie said, relieved to be able to dodge the question she wasn't quite sure how to answer.

"I'll hold you to that," said Nancy, pointing her finger at Katie, then waving as she left.

"Bye!"

Mrs. Nancy's questions stayed with Katie long after she'd escaped back into the elevator to return to her floor.

Assignments for a Season

∽

With most of the residents settled either at the arts and crafts activities or into their rooms, Katie saw Sara catch her eye and point to the break room, holding up her hand with fingers spread, meaning "in five." Perfect. They could both use a break, and it was time to catch up. They'd barely had time to say hello today.

As soon as they sat down with their coffees, Sara looked around to be sure they had some privacy. She lowered her voice but blurted it out.

"Jeremy got arrested again last night. Not just for possession this time — for dealing."

Katie didn't say a word, but got up immediately, went around the table, and hugged her friend. Sara finally let it out as the tears began to fall.

"Thanks Katie. I knew you'd get it." Sara said.

"What're you going to do?" Asked Katie.

"I don't know. Right now I'm just so mad at him, I want to wring his neck. He swore to me just last week that he was clean and even going to his meetings. What just kills me is that I believed him! Mostly, anyway. I wanted to. But it's just one more time he's lied to me. At least I didn't run down to the

Chapter 3: Getting Acquainted

jail to bail him out at three o'clock this morning. He can just sit there and think for awhile about how he's screwing up his life," she said, with more conviction than she felt. She hoped she was doing the right thing, and was searching Katie's eyes for confirmation.

Katie nodded and continued to listen as Sara poured out her hurt, fear, and disappointment, until their break was over. They both stood and hugged again, tossed their cardboard coffee cups into the trash bin, and with a big mutual sigh, went back to work. Sara and Katie had a friendship that was really special. They could tell each other anything.

Assignments for a Season

Chapter 4

Three weeks later
Going with God's Flow

"Oh, thank you, Sara. That water feels so good!" Nancy cooed, as she took her morning shower. Sara had adjusted the water's flow and temperature, and helped Nancy into the bathroom. Nancy was pretty good at transferring herself from her chair to the shower seat; she only needed a minimum amount of help. It had become a routine by now, one they both enjoyed.

Sara liked that Nancy was appreciative and didn't fight with her about taking showers like so many of the other residents. Most of the others she helped were either in the early stages of dementia, or just prideful about not being able to do everything themselves. Of course down in Memory Care, the special unit for residents with severe dementia, it sometimes took three of them to get one resident safely bathed. At home the kids might not like taking their baths, but full-grown adults who don't want to wash up are a whole other thing.

"You have no idea what a blessing you are," Nancy said, interrupting Sara's thoughts. She heard Nancy turn off the shower, signaling she'd finished. Sara handed her a towel and then her robe.

"You know when my husband Tad died, I had no idea what I would do, how I'd survive without him. I depended on him so much. And he seemed to love doting on me. I tried to live with my children. I spent three months each with two of them, and while they loved me, they really didn't feel comfortable helping me with all that I needed. Besides, they had families and routines of their own, and I was interrupting. I'm so glad God gave me this new assignment — and put you here, too, at just the right time to help me."

Sara smiled and started combing Nancy's hair. "Would you like to wear it up today?"

"No, leave it down," she said. "I'll use some hair combs, though, to keep it out of my face."

"Tell me more about this 'new assignment,'" Sara said, as she fixed Nancy's hair.

"Oh that!" Nancy laughed a little. "When I first got my chair, after the accident, I was in a bad way. My attitude was terrible.

Chapter 4: Going with God's Flow

I was mad at the world and wasn't even sure about my faith. It just felt like I'd lost everything. But God waited me out. Like a patient parent when a child is throwing a tantrum… He just waited and waited, until I was ready to listen. Tantrums are full of drama, but they don't get us anywhere."

"My little Sophia threw one of those just this morning!" Sara smiled at the memory of her stubborn six-year-old that morning, and the very idea of Mrs. Nancy having a bad attitude. She couldn't even imagine it.

"You know, dear, God speaks to each one of us differently," she said. "Do you hear His voice?"

"Well, not out loud, but I think I hear Him. Sometimes. Then there are times I wish He'd speak a little louder," Sara said, smiling. *Like what to do about Jeremy,* she continued her thought silently.

"Exactly. Well, He gave me a great big lesson in listening. He directed me to some very specific Scriptures, and some special people too. He often talks to me through other people. You know, the ones that just 'happen' along, and in talking, they give me the very answers I was looking for! He's really incredible in that way.

"That's when I realized I had my first assignment. And it was to live. Not just survive, which was a miracle that I did. But I was to live my life to the fullest, for Him. Second Corinthians four says that I may be wasting away on the outside, which was what my pity party was about. Oh, but there's more to the story! The verse goes on to say that my spirit, the part of me that is eternal, is growing stronger day by day[2]. That's an exciting thought, and one I could grab and hold onto."

Sara wheeled Nancy from her bathroom into her room and started to help her dress for the day. She had never heard anyone talk so confidently and in such detail about God before, outside church of course. Nancy seemed to have something more real about her faith, and Sara was drinking it all in as Nancy kept going.

"Then God began to show me how I could serve others, even if it was just a smile to brighten someone's day, or a little word of thanks or encouragement. I get to do a lot of people-watching. This chair makes some people look right past me as if I'm invisible. So I get to see things that others might miss when they can hurry and scurry a little more than I can.

"As I got stronger, I started going down to the elementary school and reading to the children. It gave the teachers a little break, and children are so accepting. We learned together, the children and I. God started really growing me up and deepening my faith and dependence on Him. It got to the point I felt like He was tutoring me personally — and then I realized that was exactly what He was doing!"

Nancy and Sara both laughed.

"It's just about time for breakfast," Sara said. "I hate to cut this short because I want to hear more, but I bet you're getting pretty hungry."

Chapter 4: Going with God's Flow

"Yes, I am. We will pick up here tomorrow," promised Nancy. Sara rolled her down to the dining room, as the smells of freshly cooked bacon and cinnamon muffins came wafting out of the kitchen.

∼

"Why is it I only notice that I've dropped a stitch when I'm several rows past where it dropped, and have a hole?" Kristin half fussed, half whined to Mrs. Nancy. "Then I just have to pull it all out back to the mistake."

"Kind of like life, isn't it? You have to go back to where you messed up, and fix it. But you'll get the hang of it. You're doing really well," she encouraged. "Just go a little more slowly, and you won't drop your stitches. In the long run, you'll finish faster. And you'll get faster too, with practice."

Nancy and some of the other residents were avid knitters, or "fiber artists" as they like to call themselves these days. She had offered to teach Kristin only if she'd promise to join them.

Kristin had always thought of knitting as too slow to be interesting (she held the same opinion of baseball), but decided that for Nancy, she'd give it a try. And she was pleasantly surprised. It was both more challenging and interesting than she'd assumed.

Assignments for a Season

Nancy and some of the others had all piled in the Lakeview Senior Care van and visited the hobby shop. They carefully picked out all the yarn and needles and patterns for each of their projects, including taking great interest and care in the best starter project for her. They decided she would be making a winter scarf, in shades of light blue and dark forest green.

"The blue will bring out your eyes, and the green will look great against your red hair," they had assured her.

Kristin couldn't imagine getting the project finished by winter, but she agreed, a little less than enthusiastically, to try.

Back at Lakeview, they couldn't wait to help her get started. They showed her how to roll the skeins of yarn into balls, twist a single strand around her thumb and forefinger to begin casting her first stitches onto one knitting needle, then pick up the other needle to knit and pearl according to the pattern's directions. Holding the needles and wrapping the yarn strands around her fingers felt awkward. It was the kind of girly-girl stuff that she'd always avoided, growing up with a houseful of brothers. But she wanted to build a closer relationship with the residents, and they'd been asking for this. So here she was. If her brothers could only see her now. Ha. They would laugh and tease her — and she would chase them, vowing her revenge.

"The relaxing thing about knitting," Nancy observed, speaking to no one in particular, "is that, once you learn how, of course, it forces you to slow down a little and focus deliberately, but not

Chapter 4: Going with God's Flow

too intently. Like taking a nice deep breath. There's a rhythm to it. There's always time to rush about your business later. For right now, we knit."

About that time, Katie came dashing out the Memory Care door.

"Can I get a little help here? Anyone who's available—now!"

Kristin perked up and looked around at her fellow fiber artists, and they all nodded their heads, yes, go, help her.

Mr. Walter had come out of his room stark naked, then squatted and pooped in the middle of the lobby floor. There were only two aides working in Memory Care at the time, and both were needed to accompany Mr. Walter back to his room and get him cleaned up and clothed, while a third was needed to see to the floor cleanup before anyone stepped in it.

"Thanks Kristin," Katie said. "I owe you one for this. I know it's not exactly in your job description, but we appreciate the help. Jerri's already gone for the day."

"Don't mention it. I was in way over my head trying to knit — so this is a good diversion. Want me to help you with Mr. Walter, or find the mop?"

"I'll take the mop if you can get Walter cleaned up and settled. He's pretty easy. Just remember, tell him in advance what you're doing, and go slow."

"Got it. We'll be fine." *Slow seems to be the theme of the day,* Kristin mused, remembering Mrs. Nancy's knitting advice.

After about twenty minutes, Kristin emerged from Walter's room with a satisfied smile.

"OK, Walter's all cleaned up and settled. By the way, where's Liz? Is she on her way to check him out medically?"

Katie rolled her eyes. "She's probably on the phone again with her new boyfriend. She'll be here when she's good and ready," she said, as she lifted her eyebrows and shook her head in disapproval.

"What? During work hours? I thought that was against the rules," Kristin said.

"It is." Katie answered. "For us."

Silence hung in the air for a moment as Kristin absorbed the information. Liz felt entitled to break the rules everyone else had to follow.

A few minutes later, Liz arrived and went to Walter's room to take his vitals. This wasn't typical of the Memory Care patients, but it wasn't all that unusual either. It was important to first handle the cleanup and second, check to see if there were any new symptoms surfacing that might indicate an oncoming illness or infection causing the behavior. UTIs, or Urinary Tract Infections, were legendary for prompting strangely uncharacteristic behavior in the elderly.

∼

Chapter 4: Going with God's Flow

Without any help from Sara, Jeremy managed to make bail, and the court had appointed an attorney for him, a public defender. It would be two more months before his trial. In the meantime, after sitting in jail for nearly two weeks as he got that worked out, he'd lost his welding job at the plant; he was fired for being a no-show. Without the job, he'd also lost his apartment as soon as rent came due. At least he got out in time to get his stuff before being evicted. He moved in with his mom over in Simpson, about an hour's drive from Lakeview City. He was looking at up to ten years, based on the charges against him, and with the stress of the situation, Jeremy seemed to be drinking and using more than ever, as far as Sara could tell when she talked to him. With the help of her prayer partners at work and in her support group, she started to face facts and make plans.

Being realistic, child support was going to be a thing of the past so Sara started looking for a second job. Since she was usually off on Sundays, she took a position as a paid nursery worker at her church, but that income wouldn't go far. She applied for a third-shift job at McDonald's but wondered if cleaning houses in the afternoons might pay better. She made a mental note to talk to Jerri at work tomorrow. Sara knew she moonlighted cleaning private homes after work. She'd have to talk to her sister, too, about keeping the kids.

Assignments for a Season

"Earth to Sara! Calling Sara Johnson!" Nancy said to Sara with a smile. "Sweetheart, you must have been a thousand miles away. I hope you had a good trip," she teased.

"Sorry Mrs. Nancy, you're right — I just zoned out there for a minute," Sara admitted while she was fixing Nancy's hair. "But I'm back now. Still good with the yellow pants set for today?"

"Yes, that will be fine."

"Now tell me about these God assignments you've been getting. I'm really curious, and you never got back around to explaining it," Sara said as she started helping Nancy get dressed.

"Well, you remember I told you I felt like God was tutoring me Himself — with private lessons right there in the throne room?"

"Yes."

"At that time when I was recovering, I really couldn't do anything but pray — everything else was in a cast or traction. But my dear husband and some friends from church were so good to read the Bible to me daily and pray with and for me.

"During that time, there were several verses that just seemed to jump out at me, and then get strung together. The first, as I told you, was that I was healthy and growing inside, regardless of the broken condition of my outside, 2 Corinthians 4:16. The second one was in John, chapter twelve, where Jesus talks about the fact that a seed has to die before it can grow and bear fruit. Then he says it's figuratively the same for us, that, 'whoever loves his life

Chapter 4: Going with God's Flow

loses it, and whoever hates his life in the world will keep it for eternal life.'[3] In other words, if you want to stay as you are — in this analogy, a seed, you're going to die anyway. But if you are willing to let go of the world, and be transformed by God, then He will reward you with eternal life.

"Paul reinforced the idea when he said in Second Timothy that his life was being poured out like a drink offering.[4]

"Well, I'll tell you, at that point I did hate my life. I was miserable, and I was happy to turn the whole mess over to Jesus if He could do something with it. But if He could use me to bear fruit, He was going to have to show me how. I realized that what Paul meant by pouring out his life was that he was using his life for Christ. It was his calling, and he was spending his life for it.

"Did you ever see an old classic movie called *The Sound of Music*?"

"With Julie Andrews? Yes! Loved it," Sara said. "My grandmother played it for me when I was little," she added with a giggle, "She didn't like the modern movies and cartoons I was watching."

"That's the one. There's a song that The Reverend Mother sings before she sends Julie out of the convent, called 'Climb Every Mountain.'"

"Oh yes, '…until you find your dream,'" Sara added.

"Exactly. She's describing *calling*. It will need 'all the love you can give, every day of your life for as long as you live.' Except that we don't have to work that hard to find it — unless you just like climbing mountains," she said with a wink.

Nancy wasn't done yet with telling her "assignments" story. She kept on, and Sara wanted to hear the rest of it. "Anyway, the tutoring kept going. The scripture that jumped out next was Ephesians 2:10: *For we are his workmanship, created in Christ Jesus for good works, which God prepared beforehand, that we should walk in them.*[5] Then it all clicked. Calling isn't just for pastors and teachers! We all, as Christians, are called to live for Him — and the work He puts in front of us is our calling. The people and situations He gives us are our assignments, maybe for a day and maybe for a long while, but we don't have to look any further than what's in front of us, and it's usually as simple as that.

"I already knew that Jesus lived in my heart, that I had the Holy Spirit and was adopted into the Kingdom of heaven. You know that too, don't you, dear?" Nancy stopped to ask Sara.

"Oh yes ma'am. Since I was 16."

"Good. But what I finally realized, putting all those verses together in my broken state, was that God was in charge! Not me."

"Well, yeah… but hasn't that always been true?"

"You'd have never known that from looking at my life before the accident," Nancy said seriously. "I tried to do things my way, and was always trying to be in control. I kept trying to do things *for* God, instead of realizing that we were a team, and I could quit worrying so much and start doing things *with* God. Because He's always here, whatever is in front of me is what He has for me to do. That's my assignment.

"I can't tell you how many hours I used to spend worrying what His will was when He never meant for it to be that hard. He's never surprised by what we face, or what happens to us. And He's always right there with us. So the next thing that seems like the right thing is usually what we're to do — especially if we're focused on Him and walking with Him to begin with. He guides us right in the middle of the path He wants us to follow. Even if we're in the middle of a mess!" She chuckled, shaking her head.

"I think I'm starting to see what you mean," Sara said thoughtfully, chewing over what Nancy had said, and comparing it in her mind with what she'd been taught. She knew that she, too, had spent a great deal of time in prayer, especially lately asking and pleading with God for answers about what to do about Jeremy. It seemed like Nancy was saying that God was already in charge, so she could rely on Him to work things out. But looking for extra work, which seemed like the next right thing, was probably a good idea too.

"Are you ready for breakfast?" Sara asked, suddenly realizing the time.

"Yes," said Nancy. "But if it's okay with you, I think we should pray first. May I pray for you?"

"I'd like that."

"Heavenly Father, I thank You so much for my friend Sara and the fact that we're sisters through your Son Jesus. I know that You know what she needs, Lord, and I ask You to bless her with peace, and confidence and strength to handle whatever comes her way today. Give her grace to work with us all here at Lakeview — reward her, Father, because she is such a blessing to us. And I'm sure we don't always remember to thank her, and You too, for calling her here in Your service. Thank you, Father, in Jesus' name. Amen."

Chapter 5

Everyday Service and Sacrifice

Jerri pulled up into the parking lot to drop Teresa off. "You be a good girl and work hard today, okay? Mama loves you," Jerri said to Teresa as they met the van that would take her to work.

"K. Lov'ou — bye," Teresa mumbled as she smiled at her mom, then opened the car door, skipping in a half walk, half hop down the sidewalk to meet her friends already in the van. That was her happy dance. For Teresa, it meant she was happy. Routines gave her security.

But for Jerri, Monday mornings were hard. She watched as the van pulled away. During the week Teresa lived in a group home that provided supervised "independent" living, or at least as independent as Teresa and her co-workers could be. They all felt so grown up and successful by living there. And it gave Jerri a break, but oh it was hard to let her go back again after a great family weekend when Monday morning rolled around. Still, she was proud of Teresa and how far she'd come.

When Teresa was born, Jerri couldn't believe what a beautiful child she was. She was stunned when the doctor told her Teresa had Down syndrome. How could such a perfect baby have such a life sentence? She'd thought at the time it was a tragedy. The hospital put her in touch with a support group and pointed her to an educational program for parents. Her husband refused to attend, so Jerri went on her own. Eventually, her husband came around. Thank God for that. It could have broken their marriage, but they finally adjusted and started working as a team. Jerri was determined to give Teresa every advantage she could, to help her make the best of her life. For a time, both Jerri and her husband grieved for what she called the "could have beens" of life. The dreams and aspirations they'd had for their daughter, her life, and relationships. All that changed with one diagnosis. One extra chromosome.

Some days she was still a little wistful about her expectations, but alongside that twinge of grief was the memory of all the unexpected blessings Teresa had brought into their lives. At 27, she still had that irresistible childlike wonder and an easy laugh. She had brought them such joy, was quick to give you a hug, and was very diligent and hard-working once she put her mind to something. Yes, she had been a blessing far more

Chapter 5: Everyday Service and Sacrifice

than Jerri could have imagined in those early days. That's why Mondays were so hard. She looked heavenward. *Take good care of our baby this week, Lord. She's in your hands — just as she always has been. Thank you.*

~

"You know, I think I'm finally getting the hang of this knitting thing," remarked Kristin, as she looked admiringly at her scarf in progress, which was now almost two feet long. It had taken three weeks and was probably her third time getting to that point, but finally there were no dropped stitches, no unraveling and starting over.

"I knew you'd enjoy it. I just had a feeling about you and knitting," Nancy agreed. "And you'll remember the fun you've had with us every time you wear it — you can't get that kind of satisfaction from a store-bought scarf."

"Before you know it, you'll be planning your next project," Sally chimed in. They had come such a long way since the fuss over playing cornhole. Kristin realized that she had to slow down to listen for what activities Sally was interested in, and always start with that. She was happy to help you join in, but she didn't really like to try new things at her stage of life. Or maybe ever. Kristin didn't know. But she was relieved that the cornhole incident was behind them, and that she'd obviously been forgiven.

Assignments for a Season

Kristin was starting to feel more confident in her job and more connected to each one of the residents. She no longer thought of them as a group of "seniors" to be managed, but as unique individuals, each with their own story to tell. This was actually starting to be fun, when she focused more on them and less on trying to be perfect. Some days, her plans and lists actually worked out well. Other days, they completely fell apart for one reason or another. She was learning to take either result in stride. As Nancy had reminded her on more than one occasion, "God's mercies are new every morning, and each day can be a new adventure if you allow it." Kristin was even realizing that when she prayed about it, things went better. Not perfectly of course, but better.

She may not ever get over wanting to push Sally to be a little more active. But it was nice too, to just sit with her and knit, and be her friend.

Kristin looked up in time to see Liz pull her cell phone out of her pocket and answer it. Her whole demeanor changed. She went from professional to a giggly schoolgirl in an instant. But when she saw Kristin watching her, she self-consciously lowered her voice, ducked into her office, and closed the door.

Kristin frowned. She knew all the Resident Assistants were aware that Liz wasn't sticking to the rules everyone else had to abide by. But they weren't likely to mention it to the Executive Director, Rachael. After all, Liz was their boss. As a director herself, Kristin wondered what, if anything, she should do. She'd have to think about that one.

Chapter 5: Everyday Service and Sacrifice

∽

"Susanne and John and their families are all coming to visit!" Nancy bubbled over when Sara came to get her up and dressed this morning. Eric won't make it, but it will still be a party! What do I need to do to reserve that lovely private dining room off the lobby?"

"I can talk to Rachael for you and make sure that happens," Sara assured her. "Let me write down the date. After breakfast, you can talk to Chandra, too, about the food you'd like to have. She always makes a big fuss when families come in from out of town. She understands how the right food is a big part of such a special occasion."

"Oh, I hope so," Nancy answered. "With my crew — it's likely to be lively and exciting!"

"Ah, an *assignment*," Sara corrected, reminding her of her own lessons about life.

"Yes. An assignment."

Throughout the several months now that Nancy had been at Lakeview, Sara had noticed how so many of the staff members seemed to gravitate toward her, picking up both her wise sayings and her refreshing attitude about life.

"It's never too late to start again," "Listen for what makes your heart sing," and, "God doesn't want you to get it perfectly right, He wants to get you, perfectly, in the process," were all witticisms coming out of staff members' mouths. They were often preceded by, "Mrs. Nancy says…" as they were being repeated all over the community. *Yes, I think she was right: This is Mrs. Nancy's assignment, and she's doing it well,* Sara mused. *Mine too.*

Residents and staff alike had learned that if you were having a bad day, you wanted to make sure you stopped by for a visit with Mrs. Nancy. She'd lift your spirits for sure. Mrs. Fields and Mrs. Sally were both in her bridge club on Wednesday afternoons, and even they were getting easier to get along with as they spent more time with Mrs. Nancy.

∽

Chandra Patel, the Director of Food Services, met with Nancy to plan the big day. There would be ten altogether, including Mrs. Nancy. They'd be bringing cake to celebrate her birthday, but Lakeview would provide the rest of the meal.

Nancy's excitement was contagious. She hadn't seen her children, except by computer chat, since she'd moved in. They were making a special visit to help celebrate her 85th birthday, and then Susanne and Joe's family would be traveling on to the beach. Nancy was glad she had passed on her love of the ocean to at least one of her children. Susanne loved it every bit as much as she had, in her younger, healthier days. Besides,

Chapter 5: Everyday Service and Sacrifice

Nancy knew that memories made with family last forever, and children grow so fast. It was best to make memories when they're young, or later, they won't be interested. Beach trips are a wonderful opportunity for families to blend and bond.

There would be a Southern country spread with a choice of chicken and dumplings, ham, green beans, sliced tomatoes, corn bread, and tossed salad. And birthday cake, of course. All were family favorites that had been served many times in her home as the children who were now adults had been growing up.

Chandra also offered to make sure the local florist delivered a centerpiece of hydrangeas, too. Nancy had mentioned that she loved them. It would be a very special day. What Nancy didn't know is that members of her church had already contacted Kristin, and would be coming by mid-morning with a special birthday banner and balloon bouquets. Chandra would be sure they were up in the private dining room in time for the noon celebration with her family. Everyone wanted to do whatever they could to help Nancy celebrate her birthday.

∽

"Liz, can we talk?" Kristin asked, from the doorway of Liz's office. Liz had been working on some charts just before the shift turnover meeting.

"Sure, what's up?"

Kristin took a deep breath and sat down in the office side chair. Liz kept working.

"Look Liz, I know I'm new, comparatively speaking, on the management team, and we haven't had a lot of time to talk personally," Kristin began.

"So I'm probably going to screw this up. But I've got something I need to talk to you about, and I want you to know in advance, that I'm saying this with the best of intentions, because if the situation was reversed, I'd want to know. So I'll ask for your grace and forgiveness in advance."

Wow. Liz found her defenses going up. She put her pen down and turned to face her colleague. Kristin had her full attention.

"Okay," she answered. "Let's have it."

Too late to turn back now, Kristin thought to herself. She hoped her nervousness didn't show. She hated conflict, but injustice bothered her more, and it didn't feel right to go over Liz's head speak to Rachael without talking to Liz first.

"You know how this place is like a small town. The rumor mill is pretty strong. So I can tell you that you've got a new boyfriend. That's great, and it's none of my business, I know. But as a director, you may not realize what bending the work rules about cell phones and personal calls is doing to morale. It's setting up an 'us versus them' mentality when the Resident Assistants and CNAs see you doing what they're not allowed to do. They know they wouldn't be able to get away with it

Chapter 5: Everyday Service and Sacrifice

without being written up."

Kristin took a deep breath and continued. "I know it's hard to know how you're coming across to others, and I'm sure it hasn't seemed like a big deal, but it is. If I was doing something that was undermining my leadership … well, I'd want someone to be honest enough to tell me."

Liz had listened intently, and while her cheeks were flushed, she was silent for what seemed like forever. Kristin was afraid to breathe, expecting a tirade, or denial, or some kind of response. With none coming, Kristin finally stood up.

"Well, that's all I had to say. Thanks for hearing me out." She turned to leave.

"Thank you," Liz finally replied, so quietly that Kristin barely heard her.

Neither woman ever mentioned it again. But the personal phone calls at work stopped. Kristin was naive enough to have hoped Liz would apologize to her staff, but if that happened, she never heard about it. Still, she was relieved not to have to go to Rachael with the information.

∽

"You seem to have a special zip in your step today, Jerri. What's your secret?" Nancy noticed as Jerri was cleaning her room.

"Oh I'm always happy on Fridays. As soon as I'm off, I go pick up Teresa and have her home for the weekend. I'm always on top of the world on Fridays. Monday, when I have to take her back, not as much," Jerri said.

"One thing I've learned is that life doesn't turn out the way I want it or will it. I try to take the good with the bad, and we're to thank God for both, don't you think?" Nancy said. "I'd have never chosen this chair, for instance. But God has used it —"

"Oh yes. I'm not UN-satisfied with my life. Even on Mondays. But like you, I never pictured this. Life certainly didn't turn out at all like I'd pictured."

"And sometimes, my friend, that's another reason for giving thanks!" Nancy laughed, and Jerri did too.

"Yes, ma'am. It certainly is."

∼

When the big day arrived to celebrate Nancy's birthday, all the residents with birthdays that month were invited into the lobby after breakfast, and six members of St. Matthews' Little Angels Choir came in, with a single red rose for each birthday person, and sang a rousing round of "Happy Birthday to You," followed by fruit punch and cupcakes. The choir went on to sing other songs popular with the residents, including the ever-present "You Are My Sunshine." They also delivered handmade birthday greeting cards to each celebrant.

Chapter 5: Everyday Service and Sacrifice

It started off the day on a fabulous note, before the choir members left with their parents and Kristin took over with additional activities for everyone. Celebrations like this reinforced the sense of family and home that they tried so hard to provide at Lakeview Senior Care despite the large group setting. The owners and staff were well aware that the residents had given up their private homes and familiar networks of support in order to live there. Most residents had lost a degree of their independence, and more than a little space and privacy in return for the daily assistance they needed. It was often the last home they would live in, and everyone wanted these residents to live this final life season well and comfortably, with the full knowledge that they are loved.

∽

"Now I see why you've been raving about the food here," Susanne said. "It's so nice of them to go to so much trouble so we can all celebrate together. Happy Birthday, Mom. I love you."

"Thanks Sweetie, I love you too," Nancy replied. She was glad Susanne had finally accepted her decision to move to Lakeview. It was so good to have them all here. The private dining room was nice, but nothing could beat having it brimming over with family, food, and a fun celebration, especially when there was cake coming! Susanne had made her famous fresh coconut cake, which was Nancy's favorite. Nancy couldn't imagine how Susanne had traveled all the way from Tennessee with two young children and the cake still intact, but it was beautiful and sitting on the sideboard waiting to be served. Fortunately, and at Nancy's insistence, there were no candles. "Let's not count the years, just the memories," she'd told them.

It was almost like old times, when Tad was alive, and before everything went haywire. The grandchildren looked so much like their parents. *Yes, God is certainly good*, Nancy thought as she thanked God for her happy, healthy family, and that she could be here with them.

Nancy turned her attention to little Emily, her youngest grandchild, who had just turned five. "My what a big girl you're growing up to be!" Nancy told her. "And I understand you're going to the beach this weekend — won't that be fun?"

"Uh-huh," Emily said. Her eyes were focused mainly on the cake, as her Uncle John was putting it onto the dining table for serving. They may have agreed to no candles, but they never promised not to sing. Everyone joined in, singing the Happy Birthday song as enthusiastically as they could. It was followed by a round of applause.

"Now let us eat cake!" Nancy declared. While Susanne was cutting and serving the cake, Nancy turned again to Emily.

"What are you most looking forward to when you get to the beach?" She asked Emily.

Emily thought for a minute. "The waves… And the fish…

Chapter 5: Everyday Service and Sacrifice

And going swimmin'… And seeing ALL my cousins! Even Uncle Eric!" She said with a satisfied smile, as if she'd remembered the complete list in her mind.

You could have heard a pin drop, as everyone around the table was suddenly silent. The big secret was out.

Nancy swallowed hard. No one had told her Eric would be joining them at the beach. To find out from Emily felt like a physical blow. But it wasn't the child's fault.

"Mom —" Susanne started to explain.

But Nancy recovered from her surprise and spoke up first. She waved her hand to Susanne, as if to say— not now— then turned to Emily, forced a smile and said, "Really? That's wonderful Honey. I know you're going to have a really good time. I used to love the beach when I was your age."

And with that, the party was on again. Conversation resumed, but Nancy barely tasted her cake. She told everyone she was full, and would save the rest of her piece for later.

After the festivities, Susanne volunteered to take her mother back to her room to rest. She knew they needed to talk.

"Suze, why didn't you tell me?" Nancy asked, as soon as they got in her room. "We've always been open with each other." Her tone was more filled with hurt than accusation.

"Eric made me promise not to say anything," Susanne said lamely. "We've just recently been back in touch. He told me he just can't face you yet."

"After all these years? How many times do I have to tell Eric he's forgiven? I forgive him, God forgives him — even your Dad forgave him. There should be nothing keeping him away."

"Mom, Eric hasn't forgiven himself," Susanne said softly. "We can't exactly forget what he did."

"He was so young," Nancy couldn't help herself — the tears began to flow. "We didn't understand about addiction. I had no idea what he'd gotten into, and when I got in the car with him that night, I certainly had no idea that he was high. He was still just a boy! It was an accident. Eric acts like we banished him from the family. We didn't. The consequences took some adjusting, but he didn't have to go away for all those years. I worried so much about him. And when he wrote me a letter —"

"I remember. It was before Dad died. We were all hoping Eric would come back into the family, Mom. Part of his program is to make amends; we were hoping it wouldn't stop with just taking responsibility for what he'd done and apologizing. We wanted an opening for a real relationship again. I know you did too. From what I understand he was homeless and drifted for a long time, but he finally hit bottom and got help. He lived in a group home for a couple of years and got some counseling. Now with his own place, and a steady job in software sales — he's doing so much better. He told me he's been clean and sober for six years. But Mom, Eric's afraid of what it will do to him to see you again… like this. The guilt still haunts him. Someday, he'll have to face the consequences of what he did that night. But first, baby steps. He's joining us for two days. We'll see how it goes."

Nancy was quiet for a long time. Then she shook her head slowly, as the facts were sinking in. "Shame is a powerful enemy," she said.

Susanne continued. "It's a huge step for him that he's agreed to meet us at the beach. You and Dad weren't the only ones he cut off, you know. We all lost a brother, in addition to almost losing you."

"I understand. You still should have told me."

"I know."

"Tell Eric again for me, that he's forgiven, and that I love him. The past is past, and he's my son. It would be nice if he'd start acting like it."

"Yes ma'am," Susanne said. "I'll tell him."

Assignments for a Season

Chapter 6

Challenges Come When A Family Gathers

Katie and Sara had both been in the room, clearing the table of lunch dishes, when Emily made her announcement about Eric coming to the beach. They had heard about Nancy's "prodigal" son, Eric, who had run away after falling into trouble.

But it wasn't until the birthday celebration and conversations in the following days that they put together the facts, and realized he was the cause of the accident that put Nancy in the wheelchair.

She had said she heard from or about him every few years. Her husband had even hired a private investigator once to find him, but Eric refused to come home. She never lost hope that one day, he'd come back and join the family. Occasionally she'd get a card or brief letter, letting her know that he was alive, and had moved to this city, or that one. Never with a return address or way to follow up.

As Katie and Sara both watched her, and compared notes about what they knew, they agreed: the remarkable thing continued to be her upbeat attitude on life. She had no bitterness. No blame. She just wanted to see her son again and love him.

"I can tell you, if one of my kids caused an accident like that, and then ran away like her son did, I think the staying away part would hurt the most," Sara told Katie one day as they talked over their lunch break.

"It's such a shame. She's so loving and forgiving," Katie said. "That would almost make it harder."

"It shows you never know what people have been like or been through before they come here," said Sara. "If I'd been through all of that, I'd be a *lot* crankier!"

They both laughed in agreement and cleaned up their dishes to get ready to go back to work.

Chapter 6: Challenges Come When a Family Gathers

During the next several days after her birthday, Nancy didn't have much of an appetite. Who could blame her? The family "reunion" she'd gone through would throw anyone off a bit. But when a few days turned into nearly two weeks, Chandra, the Food Services Director, noticed and got worried.

"Mrs. Nancy has always been one of my biggest fans," she told Liz. "She loves my cooking. Now, she barely eats a thing. It's more than just being upset about her family."

"I'll check into it," Liz assured her. "We'll get to the bottom of it." Liz made a note to check Nancy's vitals and schedule a routine appointment with her physician in the next few days.

Katie and Sara came to Liz as well. They'd noticed she had a small cough — not bad, and no fever, but she just didn't seem to be quite herself lately.

"At first, I thought she was just mourning her relationship with her son after the visit she'd had from the rest of the family," Sara explained. "But with this cough added into the mix, I'm not so sure. Of course she never complains, so how are we going to know?"

Liz paid a visit to Nancy and suggested they check her weight. She'd lost six pounds since last month.

"How's your appetite, Mrs. Nancy?" She asked.

"Oh, fine. I'm maybe not quite as hungry as I used to be. But Chandra is a great cook. It's certainly nothing to do with her food."

"Are you having any pain anywhere?"

"No, just the usual aches and pains of old age — 85 isn't for spring chickens, you know," Nancy joked. But somehow, Liz could tell, her heart wasn't quite in it like it usually was. They'd been talking now for a good 15-20 minutes and Nancy hadn't brought up a single scripture verse, which was unlike her.

She checked the schedule, and Nancy had an appointment with her physician in about 10 more days. Whatever was going on with her could probably wait until then, but she was going to call his office for a phone consult, just to be sure.

In the meantime, she brought up Mrs. Nancy during the shift change meeting, and asked that they pray for her. "Anyone living in a wheelchair is more prone to additional health issues," she explained, "and Mrs. Nancy is a breast cancer survivor, which puts her doubly at risk. So we just want to keep her in peak health. Let's keep a special eye on her over the next few days."

Chapter 7

Finishing Well

"Mrs. Nancy, you're one of the smartest women I know. Can I ask you for some advice?" Katie said, as she was brushing Nancy's hair, and helping her get ready for bed.

"I don't know about that," she laughed. "But I'll try."

"How do you know when to forgive someone and let things go? And if you're supposed to forgive them, how do you do that?"

"Well, that's kind of a big one, isn't it? First, do you understand the difference between forgiving and forgetting?"

"I think so. But aren't we supposed to forgive and forget?"

"Not entirely. The Bible commands us to forgive, just as we have been forgiven. That's the simple part. Not easy, mind you — but simple. Always forgive. Over and over, forgive. Forgiving means that you don't hold anything against them in your heart. Forgiving isn't for the other person's benefit, it's for yours. Have you ever heard that refusing to forgive someone is like drinking poison and expecting the other person to die?"

Katie laughed. "No, I don't think I've ever heard that before."

"It is funny, but it's exactly what happens when we let what the Bible calls a root of bitterness grow.[6] It can cause all kinds of trouble. So forgive, and don't let bitterness toward another person grow in your heart.

"But that doesn't mean being a doormat, either. There are consequences to actions. Personal boundaries to enforce, and so forth. Jesus told his disciples to go out into the world being wise as serpents and innocent as doves.[7] So you are to honor your relationship with God by forgiving, but He expects you to be wise about your future actions. You can't always act like trespasses never happened. But you can't keep bringing them up, either.

"Can you tell me a little more about what prompted your question?" Nancy finally asked.

Katie let out a big sigh. "My boyfriend."

"I see." Nancy asked a few more questions. Katie's answers revealed a fair amount of significant verbal abuse, and her fear

Chapter 7: Finishing Well

that it might turn physical.

"Sometimes, he's just the sweetest guy on the planet. But other times — he's a real jerk. I have a hard time with that. And he's finally talking about getting married. But I'm not even sure if I want that anymore. Do you think I'm just not forgiving him? That's what he says. He said if I really forgave him, that it wouldn't matter."

"And what do you think?" Nancy asked.

"That I want to get married and have children and a family … but that he's probably not the one. I can't see myself being able to forgive him that much," Katie said.

"Oh, you can forgive him," said Nancy. "But that's not really the issue. Consider, as you go forward — if you go forward, whether or not it's wise to put yourself in a position to be treated like that. Dear child, remember you are royalty — a daughter of the King! You deserve someone who recognizes that, and who honors you, loves you, and treats you with respect. Someone you can respect in return. Do you think he is someone like that? Because that's the real question. Pray about that one. And I'll pray for you too."

Nancy skipped the weekly fiber artists' meeting that week because she had a bad headache, an unusual complaint for her. She told Kristin that she was going back to her room to rest, in hopes it would pass, but that she was thrilled to see Kristin's good progress on her scarf.

"You're almost finished!" Nancy said, full of pride in her protégée. "You've done a really nice job on it." Then she retreated to her room. She skipped dinner that night, too.

Kristin and Sara both went to Liz. "Have you checked on Mrs. Nancy?" Sara asked her. Kristin told her about Nancy's headache.

"I peeked in her door a few minutes ago, and she was asleep," Sara reported.

"For now, I'll let her sleep," said Liz. "She's got an appointment for a checkup with her doctor tomorrow. But Sara, why don't you fix a plate for her since she missed dinner, in case she wakes up in the night and is hungry."

When the morning shift transition meeting was held, they all prayed for Mrs. Nancy. Something wasn't right. They prayed it was nothing serious.

∽

A few days later, the results from Nancy's tests were in. Her cancer was back. She'd need to see her oncologist next to find out the extent of the disease.

Chapter 7: Finishing Well

∼

Nancy's daughter drove in from Tennessee to go with her mother to the oncologist appointment in Greenville. Everyone's worst fears were realized. The cancer metastasized, aggressively. It had spread to her lungs, spine, and brain.

Susanne asked to speak to the doctor privately. "How much time do you think she has left?" She asked him.

"Only in the movies can they tell you that with any accuracy," he replied, shaking his head. "But given her condition, and the rapid weight loss, I'd say maybe a few months. Maybe less."

He made arrangements for Nancy to return to Lakeview under hospice care. Susanne called her mom's pastor, as well as Liz, to let everyone know what was going on.

"Mom doesn't want any further treatments besides palliative care," she explained. "She's been through chemo and radiation treatments before and isn't willing to do it again. She said she's lived a good life and is ready. And honestly, I think it's too late for any of those treatments to be effective now."

Susanne and the hospice nurse came to visit daily, as did her pastor. There was also a steady flow of visitors from her church.

∼

"Mrs. Quinn, have they told you what's going on?" Pastor Mark asked Nancy when he visited that first day after the diagnosis.

"Yes, Pastor," she answered. "Just about 'Amen' time, I believe." She smiled at the thought. She was glad that now they knew what was happening, she didn't even have to get out of bed. No one expected anything more of her. All of her famous assignments were nearly finished. She had a long visit with Pastor Mark. They talked and reminisced and prayed. He promised to come back again tomorrow.

She appreciated all the visitors and well-wishers, but she finally asked Susanne to give her time to sleep. She was tired. "You're probably exhausted yourself, Honey. Why don't you take some time to go rest? I'll be fine," Nancy said as she closed her eyes.

Susanne decided her mother was right. She told Sara she'd be back in the morning. No more visitors today, please.

A few hours later, Sara tip-toed into Mrs. Nancy's room, just to check and make sure she was okay, and didn't need anything. She'd learned to enter and leave residents' rooms without making a sound so she didn't disturb them if they were sleeping.

"Goodness, Sara, why are you looking so sad?" Nancy asked, catching Sara looking in on her.

They smiled at each other as Sara came over to the bed and took Nancy's hand in hers. "You know you're my favorite. I'm

Chapter 7: Finishing Well

going to miss you more than words can say," Sara told her, tears welling up in her eyes.

"I know." Nancy said. "But I'm ready to go. It has been wonderful here, but it's time to go. I'm going to see my Jesus." Nancy smiled the biggest and most peaceful smile that Sara had seen in quite some time. Yes, Sara realized. Nancy was at peace with all that was happening.

Working in a community like this, you see more than your fair share of folks face their own death. It takes courage. It was clear to Sara that Mrs. Nancy was at peace with her God and her life. Nothing was left undone that needed to be done.

It wasn't that way with everyone. Some residents fought and fussed every step of the way. Not Mrs. Nancy. She surrendered gracefully.

A few weeks later, she slipped into a coma-like semi-conscious state. Her family and friends were with her as her breathing became more labored, and more and more time passed between each breath, until she was embraced in the arms of her Savior. She was gone.

Eric had never come to see her, but she had left one more letter for him, clarifying her love and forgiveness. She'd left it with Susanne to pass on to him.

Knowing Mrs. Nancy was no longer bound to her chair, Sara liked to imagine her dancing with Jesus, and reunited with Tad and Winston. Well done, good and faithful servant.

Assignments for a Season

Chapter 8

Sara's Thoughts

Any death is a shock, Sara realized, no matter how much you might have known it was coming. I don't think you can brace yourself for it or steel yourself against its impact. It will knock you down.

But as Mrs. Nancy reminded me on several occasions, especially toward the end of her life, Jesus conquered death. And we are in Him, seated with Him in our heavenly home, she always said, Sara remembered as she tried to process her loss.

That's good news for when we cross over to be with Him, but in the here and now, I'd have to say that it's still so hard. And I know that's where faith comes in. From what I've seen of families of residents that have passed on, losing a loved one can alternately grow your faith, crush it, or cause you to question it. I choose to grow. As I look around at my co-workers, I think they choose faith-growth as well. And for many of them, I give credit to Mrs. Nancy's influence. Her faith never wavered, and it was an amazing example to us all.

Faith that even when the world doesn't make sense, God does. Faith that said, "I may not understand His plan, but He does, and He's in charge. And that's enough."

I can tell you there was a time when that certainly wasn't enough for me. I had to try and control everything, with a prepared plan A, B and C. I've learned to hold onto life more loosely because of Mrs. Nancy, and let my spirit (and those around me) breathe.

I see her influence in Kristin, who before she came to work here, rarely thought about her faith or what she believed. She used to say she missed out on the "girly girl" genes, or that they were beaten out of her by her four brothers. She didn't trust easily and was pretty closed down emotionally. Today, she's learned to open up, to let people get close to her and walk with her. It's incredible to watch her grow. Mrs. Nancy saw that love in her and brought it out. Like a dandelion in the wind, she blew Kristin's fears and doubts away, and infused her with Christ's love and trust. "I will never leave you or forsake you," was a verse Mrs. Nancy brought out just for Kristin. And let me tell you, I've seen Kristin be just as girly as any of us.

Chapter 8: Sara's Thoughts

Katie's another one that Mrs. Nancy focused on. How many times did I try to get her to drop her deadbeat boyfriend? She deserves so much better. But if he said the moon was made of green cheese, she'd believe it. I promise you, she was an otherwise bright, intelligent woman. But until Mrs. Nancy started tutoring Katie with lessons she said God Himself had passed on to her, years before — well Katie just didn't see her own value, much less stand up for it to the boyfriend. Praise God, I think she's breaking up with him tonight.

∽

After appeals and delays, Jeremy was sentenced to six years in prison. *They take drug dealing pretty seriously here in North Carolina. I've got to say, even with no child support and having to work two jobs, life has become much more "drama free" since his departure. Our divorce will be final next Spring. I'll probably always love him. But unless and until he can prove to me he's clean and would be a good father — well, I'll just have to leave that one up to God. My assignment is to raise our kids, keep them as safe as I can, and love on the residents of Lakeview and take care of them too.*

Mrs. Nancy always talked about God's assignments for her. I think we were her assignment. Her last great legacy was pouring her life into the 60-odd community members and staff here at Lakeview. Like an Apostle from biblical times, she made us believe that we were wonderful — because we are. We are made in the image of God, and she never forgot to remind us of that, which is pretty remarkable when you think about the work so many of us do here. We love the elderly residents and wash way more than their feet. We change the sheets and do the laundry, and sometimes we wrestle them into showers and their clothes. We slow down to help them walk to the dining room, and clean up messes generated from and deposited onto every body part imaginable. It isn't glamorous.

Mrs. Nancy seemed to look past all that. She saw that most of us here have been adopted into the family of the Living God, and as such, are sons and daughters of the King. That's pretty darn special. We were sometimes the ones who forgot, in the daily "doingness" of life. We were working so hard, we'd sometimes forgotten to look up, to the One who made us all, the One that we'd determined to serve in the first place.

I can see touches of Mrs. Nancy all over this place, and in the hearts of all of us here. She is here, and yet will be sorely missed. Thank you, Lord Jesus, for bringing Mrs. Nancy here on her last assignment.

Susanne sent a letter after the funeral. It was mailed to Rachael, but addressed to the whole staff. In the letter of thanks from Susanne, there was also one last tutorial from Mrs. Nancy. Susanne had found it among her mother's things. It was full of gratitude and thanks.

"I've heard it said that, 'Those who have given of themselves to others, will live forever in every single heart they have

Chapter 8: Sara's Thoughts

touched.' Thank all of you, for touching my heart. I know that your reward will be great, for you have all stored up treasure in heaven with your wonderful care for me. Let your hearts be there in heaven as well. I'll be waiting to see you again."

Yes, I've thought a lot about my friend Mrs. Nancy since her passing. She took life in with such ease and grace. I think we'd all be better off if we slowed down just a little, and took our lead from her.

Before Jeremy and I married, I worked in housekeeping for a fancy golf resort. It sounded so cool to tell people I worked there. It was glamorous, frequented by celebrities, and the work was of relative ease compared to Lakeview... But what I learned there is that most of us live pretty ordinary lives, regardless of how fancy they may sound or look from the outside. We're all rushing around, just trying to survive and make life work. What I learned from Mrs. Nancy was how quickly it can all go away, and that most of what we strive for and call success isn't what really matters. It's all temporary. The only thing really worth experiencing is loving and being loved. Yet sometimes, we hardly give that part of life a second thought.

Mrs. Nancy had learned what really mattered in life. And thanks to her, I've learned it too. Now I guess my next assignment is to show that lesson to others.

Assignments for a Season

Epilogue

The staff at Lakeview Senior Care carried on, supporting one another just a little bit better for having known and loved Mrs. Nancy. If you were to sit down with any one of them for a cup of coffee and a good visit, they'd eventually get around to asking you: What's *your* assignment? Have you embraced it yet?

Assignments for a Season

About the Author

Debbie Patrick is a writer, ghostwriter, and editor at Vision Run Publishing. She has worked in broadcasting, advertising, and magazine publishing including Esquire Magazine Group, Bahakel Communications, and Raycom Sports Network. Her writing credits include having ghostwritten four books, edited dozens more, and served as a local columnist and stringer for the Knoxville News Sentinel. *Assignments for a Season* is her second credited book. She lives in Knoxville, Tennessee.

Assignments for a Season

Dominion Senior Living

Excellent service through faith and compassion.

At Dominion Senior Living we employ a unique faith-based, culture-first model to provide an engaging work environment for employees and superior satisfaction for our residents. We believe Dominion Senior Living has a unique and irreplaceable culture defined by our commitment to God, our residents, and each other. Our desire to create visionary senior living communities where we enable our team members to serve our residents and each other is the driving force behind our company and our success.

Our supportive work environment and our investments in our team members are evidence of Dominion Senior Living's commitment to creating an excellent corporate culture. Through our working environment and our career pathways, we cultivate team members who deliver the quality care that our residents and families rely on daily.

The **#DominionDifference**: Our Families, Residents, and Team Members choose us because they have FAITH that we will follow through on our commitment to honor God through our service to seniors.

We uphold this commitment through our vision to honor God through service to seniors, our mission to provide communities and services where spiritual, emotional, and physical needs of seniors are met and exceeded through an excellent staff and hospitable environment, and F.A.I.T.H. values.

F.A.I.T.H. values encapsulate the way we walk out the themes of hospitality, gratitude, love, kindness, generosity, honesty, responsibility, creativity, relationships, mission and balance:

Family: We create places where residents and team members can be part of a community that gives them a sense of security, belonging, and purpose. (Hospitality). We are committed to creating a family atmosphere by treating our team members and residents as we would our own family. We offer an environment that our residents can truly call home.

Attitude: We express our thankfulness externally through positivity and joy for the work we are fortunate to do (Gratitude). We incorporate the fruit of the spirit through our workplace culture and bless those around us by providing service with a smile (LOVE model). We express kindness and patience with each other and our residents, seeking out ways to serve and love our residents with verbal communication and personal encounters (Kindness).

Integrity: We fulfill our calling to serve seniors with the utmost integrity and respect for the work in which we have been entrusted (Generosity). We connect our lives to our mission and devote our time, our talent, and our treasures to the greater goodwill of the organization (Generosity).

Transparency: We are transparent in our business endeavors from the top down in our leadership model and across our entire portfolio because we believe in self-reflection and the opportunity it provides for us to grow. We tell the truth in everything we do. We do not participate in half-truths or intentional deceptions (Honesty). We take responsibility for challenges throughout our organization (Responsibility) and find new and better ways to solve problems and overcome challenges (Creativity).

Holistic: We serve and love our residents (Relationships) through meeting their spiritual, emotional, nutritional, and physical needs by providing a holistic approach to caring for our seniors (Mission). We commit to live our lives with intentionality towards body, mind, and spirit to serve others from an abundant overflow (Balance).

There's something really special about Dominion residences, whether they are for independent living, assisted living, Memory Care, or respite care. If you'd like to know more, visit us at:

DominionSeniorLiving.com

Endnotes

1   John 16:33 (ESV)
2   2 Corinthians 4:16 (CEV): We never give up. Our bodies are gradually dying, but we ourselves are being made stronger each day.
3   John 12:24-26 (ESV): Truly, truly I say to you, unless a grain of wheat falls into the earth and dies, it remains alone; but if it dies, it bears much fruit. Whoever loves his life loses it, and whoever hates his life in this world will keep it for eternal life. If anyone serves me, he must follow me; and where I am, there will my servant be also. If anyone serves me, the Father will honor him.
4   2 Timothy 4:6-8 (ESV): For I am already being poured out as a drink offering, and the time of my departure has come. I have fought the good fight, I have finished the race, I have kept the faith. Henceforth there is laid up for me the crown of righteousness, which the Lord, the righteous judge, will award to me on that day, and not only to me but also to all who have loved his appearing.
5   Ephesians 2:10 (ESV).
6   Hebrews 12:15 (NAS): See to it that no one comes short of the grace of God; that no root of bitterness springing up causes trouble, and by it many be defiled;
7   Matthew 10:16 (ESV): Behold, I am sending you out as sheep in the midst of wolves, so be wise as serpents and innocent as doves.

Assignments for a Season